Postman Pat
and the Tuba

Story by John Cunliffe
Pictures by Ray Mutimer

Based on the TV and Video Special
designed by Ivor Wood

André Deutsch · Children's Books ·

Look out for:
Postman Pat and the Toy Soldiers
Postman Pat Takes the Bus
Postman Pat and the Barometer
Postman Pat and the Toy Soldiers Sticker Book
Postman Pat Takes the Bus Sticker Book
Postman Pat and the Tuba Sticker Book
Postman Pat and the Barometer Sticker Book

Scholastic Children's Books
Scholastic Publications Ltd,
7-9 Pratt Street, London NW1 0AE

Scholastic Inc.,
555 Broadway, New York, NY 10012-3999, USA

Scholastic Canada Ltd,
123 Newkirk Road, Richmond Hill,
Ontario, Canada, L4C 3G5

Ashton Scholastic Pty Ltd,
PO Box 579, Gosford, New South Wales,
Australia

Ashton Scholastic Ltd,
Private Bag 92801, Penrose, Auckland
New Zealand

First published by Scholastic Publications Ltd 1994
Text copyright © John Cunliffe 1994
Illustrations copyright © Scholastic Publications Limited and
Woodland Animations Limited 1994

ISBN: 0 590 54164 1

Typeset by Rapid Reprographics
Printed by Proost International Book Production

10 9 8 7 6 5 4 3 2 1

It's been a quiet week in Greendale.

Nothing much happened.

Pat trimmed his hedge on Monday.

It rained on Tuesday.

Miss Hubbard bought a new hat on Wednesday.

Alf's cow had a calf on Thursday.

That was about all the news. A *quiet* week.

"What a sleepy old place," said Pat.

"*Boring!*" said Katy and Tom.

And then something happened that woke everyone up. It all began with a poster in the post-office. It said:

with pictures of roundabouts, and balloons, and stalls all round the words.

Everyone was full of ideas for the fête.

"We must have lots of stalls," said the Reverend Timms.

"Swings and roundabouts," said Katy and Tom.

"Jam and cakes," said Dorothy Thompson.

"There's plenty in my attic," said Granny Dryden, "for two or three stalls."

And when Pat called with the letters, she said, "Do climb up, Pat, and have a look."

So that's what Pat did.

"What have you found?" called Granny Dryden, from the bottom of the ladder.

"Atishooooooo!" said Pat, "Dust ...and...atishoooooo...more dust!"

"What else?"

"Hats and bats; boxes and bulging bags. Oh, and...*this*...!"

"What is it?"

"Ummmm...I'm not sure. Looks like part of a ship. A big round brassy thing..."

"Oh, Pat, it's nothing to do with a ship, it's…"

"BOOOOOOOM!"

"Pat, are you all right?"

"Yes, I just blew into it. I've found out what it is. It might sound like a ship, but it's... well, an ooomph-pah thing for a band."

"A tuba!" cried Granny Dryden, laughing. "My old dad used to play it at the village fête, years and years ago."

"Wouldn't it be great," said Pat, "to have a real live band at the fête once more. I'd love to play this old tuba."

"Then it's yours," said Granny Dryden. "A present. But you'll have to learn how to play it."

"Well," said Pat, "I played a bugle when I was a boy, in the scouts."

"This is a lot bigger," said Granny Dryden.

"And it takes a lot more puff," said Pat, "but I'll have a go, I certainly will."

13

Pat was on his way. But, he just couldn't resist having a go with the tuba. He stopped in a quiet place, got the tuba out, and blew into it with all his might.

BLAAAAAAAAAAAAAHHHHHHHHHHHHH!

Oh, what a dreadful noise it made! Jess shot up a tree, a chimney-pot fell off at Greendale Farm, and all the rabbits for two miles bolted down their holes.

"Oh dear," said Pat, putting the tuba away again. It took half an hour to get Jess out of that tree.

Peter Fogg passed on his motorbike, with his guitar slung across his back.

Ted had a mouth-organ.

At the school, the children were practising on their recorders.

When Pat called on
Miss Hubbard, the sound
of her old piano came
from the back parlour.

"There's a lot of music in Greendale," said Pat to Jess. "But none of them make a noise like that old tuba. Now, I wonder where I can get a bit of practising in, where no-one will hear?"

Strange things happened in Greendale during the weeks that
followed. Weird sounds were heard all over the valley. Strange
moanings and groanings; sudden wails and squeaks; deep booming
sounds, that vibrated and shook the walls of the houses.

PC Selby was riding his bike along a quiet road one day. As he passed Ted's truck, there was a sudden BLAAAAAARRRRRRTTTTTT that made him fall off his bike. He landed in a bed of nettles in the ditch.

A FLLLLOOOOOOMMMMBBBBBB in the village street made Mrs Pottage drop all her shopping.

A sudden GGGLLLLLLUUUUUUMMMFFFFF made Alf think he had a puncture.

21

And at Thompson Ground, a great shrieking SSSCCCCRRRRRROOOOOOOOFFMMM sent the hens and ducks and geese running in all directions, and brought Dorothy out with the pitchfork, looking for robbers.

Greendale was no longer the quiet place it had once been. What was going on? Was it ghosts? Was it flying-saucers? A secret aircraft being tested? No, it was none of these. It was Pat practising on his tuba. And, when PC Selby and the Reverend Timms caught him one night, in a field behind the church, Pat said, "I just wanted to practise. I thought no-one would hear me..."

"Now, then," said PC Selby, "this won't do, Pat, giving folks a fright."

"Nonsense," said Reverend Timms, "Pat only wants to make music. Most commendable. Now, Pat, why don't you pop along to see Major Forbes? He used to play the...ermmm...tuba, in the army band. I'm sure he could give you a few lessons. You never know, we might have a tune from you for the village fête. That would be wonderful."

"That's a great idea, Reverend," said Pat.

The very next day, Pat did as the Reverend had suggested. The
Major was delighted to see Pat. He turned out all his old music, and
they set to work there and then. There were still more strange sounds
for Greendale to suffer. The windows of Garner Hall shook with
many a BOOOOMMM and BRUMPHHH but as time went by, the
sounds grew gentler, turning into a regular OOMPH-PAH OOMPH-
PAH. Old tunes came drifting across the fields. People began to stop
to listen, and smile, and tap their feet. Pat was making real music at
last!

And then other plans were afoot. More people began arriving at Garner Hall. Peter with his guitar. Katy and Tom with their recorders. Miss Hubbard, with a bundle of books under her arm. The sounds of music swelled larger and larger from the windows of Garner Hall.

Then came the time for the fête. When all the stalls were ready, Ted fixed up the old record-player, as he said, "Just in case we need it."

But it blew a valve in the middle of the first record, and there was no way of mending it.

"Forward the New Greendale Mixed Band," said the Major.

With a proud OOMPH-PAH OOMPH-PAH, Pat led the band out from the village hall, playing with all their might.

"I've brought my mouth organ," said Ted, "mind if I join in?"

"All welcome!" roared the Major. "With a one...two...three..."

And the band let fly with all its might and main. What a noise it made! But, it got better and better as the afternoon wore on.

"Just like the old days, when I was a lass," said Granny Dryden.
"Isn't it just grand."

31

The fête was a tremendous success. When it was all over, and everything had been packed away, it seemed so peaceful.

"Well," said Pat, "it's nice to be quiet. *Sometimes!*"